bitty ☆ baby
at the ballet

by Kirby Larson
& Sue Cornelison

☆American Girl®

Special thanks to Dr. Laurie Zelinger, consultant,
child psychologist, and registered play therapist.
Dr. Zelinger reviewed and helped shape the "For Parents"
section, which was written by editorial staff.

Questions or comments? Call 1-800-845-0005,
visit **americangirl.com,** or write to Customer Service,
American Girl, 8400 Fairway Place, Middleton, WI 53562-0497.

Printed in China
13 14 15 16 17 18 19 20 LEO 10 9 8 7 6 5 4 3 2 1

Series Editorial Development: Jennifer Hirsch & Elizabeth Ansfield
Art Direction and Design: Gretchen Becker
Production: Tami Kepler, Judith Lary, Paula Moon, Kristi Tabrizi

I pulled on my tights and sparkly tutu. I helped Bitty Baby with her costume, too.

"I'm ready for the recital," I told Mommy. "Watch this!"

Bitty Baby and I did the butterfly dance

Twirl, twirl,
step, step,
point.

We didn't make one mistake.

Mommy clapped. "Bravo!" she said.
"Miss Patti will be so proud."

At the recital hall, Miss Patti called us over to the barre and told us to sit, crisscross applesauce. Then she passed around a paper sack. "Pick out a smile to wear onstage," she said.

Miss Patti likes playing pretend, just like me! I picked out a big smile. So did Bitty Baby.

"Follow me, little butterflies," said Miss Patti. We flittered and fluttered behind her. "Here is your garden," she said. "Find a flower to sit on while you wait for your turn to dance."

Bitty Baby and I sat
on a pink flower near
the curtain.

"It won't be long now,"
said Miss Patti.

Bitty Baby and I
peeked through an
opening in the curtain.

"Look at all those people!"
I whispered.

My stomach did a somersault

"I can't see Mommy and Daddy," said Bitty Baby.

I scooted back. "I didn't know there would be so many mommies and daddies," I said.

"Too many!" said Bitty Baby.

"What if I forget my steps?" I asked.
"With all those people watching!"

Bitty Baby looked as if she
might cry. We hugged
each other tight.

"I think a story would be a good idea," I said.
"Do you?"

Bitty Baby nodded. "One with no dancing."

"No dancing," I agreed. I started the story.

Once there was a
bunny who was a
very good hopper.
She always landed,
hippity-hop, right
on her tippy-toes. But
Bunny did not like to hop
in front of strangers.

One day, Bunny heard about a hopping contest.

"You should enter," said her mommy.

"You would win!" cheered her seven brothers and sisters. "You're the best hopper in the meadow."

They talked her into it.

You can do it!

On the day of the contest, Bunny
hip-hopped over the meadow flowers.
She wiggled through the brambles

and popped out on the other side.
There were rabbits everywhere! Bunny
couldn't move. Not even one little flick of her ear.

"I didn't know so many bunnies would be watching me," said Bunny. She hopped back to the meadow. Bitty Baby was in the meadow, too, playing hide-and-seek with a butterfly.

"Do you want to play with us?" asked Bitty Baby.

Bunny's ears drooped. "No, thank you," she said. "I'm too jumpy to play."

"Jumpy?" asked Bitty Baby.

"I want to be in the hopping contest, but I can't hop in front of all those strangers," said Bunny.

Bitty Baby thought for a minute
"Is it because you haven't
practiced?" she asked.

"I practice every
day," said Bunny.

"Do you have trouble landing on your tippy-toes?" asked Bitty Baby.

"No, I do it every time! Watch." Bunny showed off her best jumps.

"You *are* a good hopper!" said Bitty Baby. "Good enough to win a prize."

"Not with everyone watching," said Bunny. Her nose twitched sadly.

"I have a question," said Bitty Baby. "Are you as good at pretending as you are at hopping?"

"Yes!" said Bunny. "Sometimes I pretend I'm an astronaut.

Sometimes I pretend I'm a teacher.

And sometimes I pretend I'm a lion."

Bitty Baby nodded. "What if you enter the contest and pretend that you are hopping for just one special friend—like me?"

"Do you think I could do that?" Bunny asked.

"Why don't you give it a try," said Bitty Baby.

At the contest, Bunny's tummy did some hopping of its own. Then she saw someone waving at her. It was Bitty Baby!

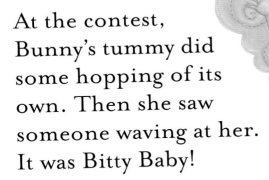

Bunny's tummy settled down. When it was her turn, she pretended she was hopping only for Bitty Baby. Bunny did her best, hippity-skippity-hopping all over the meadow. She even won a prize. The end.

"I like the way that story turned out," said Bitty Baby.

"Me, too," I said.

Miss Patti clapped her hands. "It's almost time for the butterfly dance," she said.

Mommy came to get Bitty Baby. "We'll be sitting right in front," she promised.

I tippy-toed onto the stage. Then I stopped. All those people, looking at me! My tummy started hippity-hopping like a bunny.

Bunny! I thought about Bunny and the hopping contest.

Then I took a deep breath and looked for Bitty Baby. I pretended I was dancing just for her.

Twirl, twirl, step, step, point.

When the butterfly dance was finished, all the mommies and daddies clapped. Very loud!

Bitty Baby gave me a hug.
"You are a good dancer," she said.

I hugged her back. "And you are
a good watcher."

Together, we twirled and
stepped and pointed all the way
to the ice cream parlor.

For Parents

Children love pursuing their
interests and talents, and it's
wonderful when they can take
classes to get better at something
they enjoy, whether it's dance,
music, sports, or other skills. But
sometimes your child may discover
that pursuing an interest requires
skills she hasn't yet developed, just
as learning to dance also involves
learning to perform. You can help
her gain skill and comfort, no
matter what challenges she faces.

Show her the value of her talents

- Ask her to teach you something
  you don't know how to do, such
  as play a computer game or sing
  a song that she learned at school.
  Point out that it's difficult to do
  something for the first time, so
  she'll need to be patient with you!

- At holidays and birthdays,
  encourage your child to give
  gifts from the heart, such as a
  dance she performs in her ballet
  costume, a picture she made, or
  a treat she helped to prepare.
  Family members will receive a
  priceless gift, and your child will
  receive something, too—a boost
  of confidence in herself and her
  abilities.

Talents can be taught by friends—and shared. Can her sister teach her a few karate kicks? Can a classmate help her learn to count to ten in Spanish? Role-play ways that she can ask people to teach her something new, and ways that she can thank them afterward—perhaps by sharing a talent of her own.

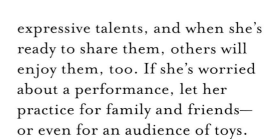

Help her shine, even if she's feeling shy

If your daughter experiences stage fright or shyness, don't pressure her. Let her know that you appreciate and enjoy her expressive talents, and when she's ready to share them, others will enjoy them, too. If she's worried about a performance, let her practice for family and friends—or even for an audience of toys.

- Visit the place she'll be performing in, so she'll feel comfortable there on the big day.

- Remind your daughter that she has done hard things before, and when she challenges herself, she is building her "confidence muscle."

  - Take her to see a performance, such as a school play or music recital. Admiring other young performers helps kids aspire to be like them.

For more parent tips, visit **americangirl.com/BittyParents**